W9-BMC-612

schwartz & wade books · new york

Central Islip Public Library
33 Hawthorne Avenue
Central Islip NY 11722-2498

3 1800 00280 3274

For Artemis

Jacket art and interior illustrations copyright © 2011 by Chris Raschka
All rights reserved. Published in the United States by Schwartz & Wade Books,
an imprint of Random House Children's Books, a division of Random House, Inc., New York.
Schwartz & Wade Books and the colophon are trademarks of Random House, Inc.
Visit us on the Web! www.randomhouse.com/kids
Educators and librarians, for a variety of teaching tools, visit us at www.randomhouse.com/teachers
Library of Congress Cataloging-in-Publication Data
Raschka, Christopher. A ball for Daisy / Chris Raschka.—1st ed. p. cm.
Summary: A wordless picture book about all the fun a dog can have with her ball.
ISBN 978-0-375-85861-1 (trade) — ISBN 978-0-375-95861-8 (glb)
[1. Dogs—Fiction. 2. Balls—Fiction. 3. Stories without words.] I. Title.
PZ7.R1814Bal 2011 [E]—dc22 2010024132
The illustrations in this book were rendered in ink, watercolor, and gouache.
MANUFACTURED IN CHINA
10 9 8 7 6 5 4 3 2 1
First Edition
Random House Children's Books supports the First Amendment and celebrates the right to read.

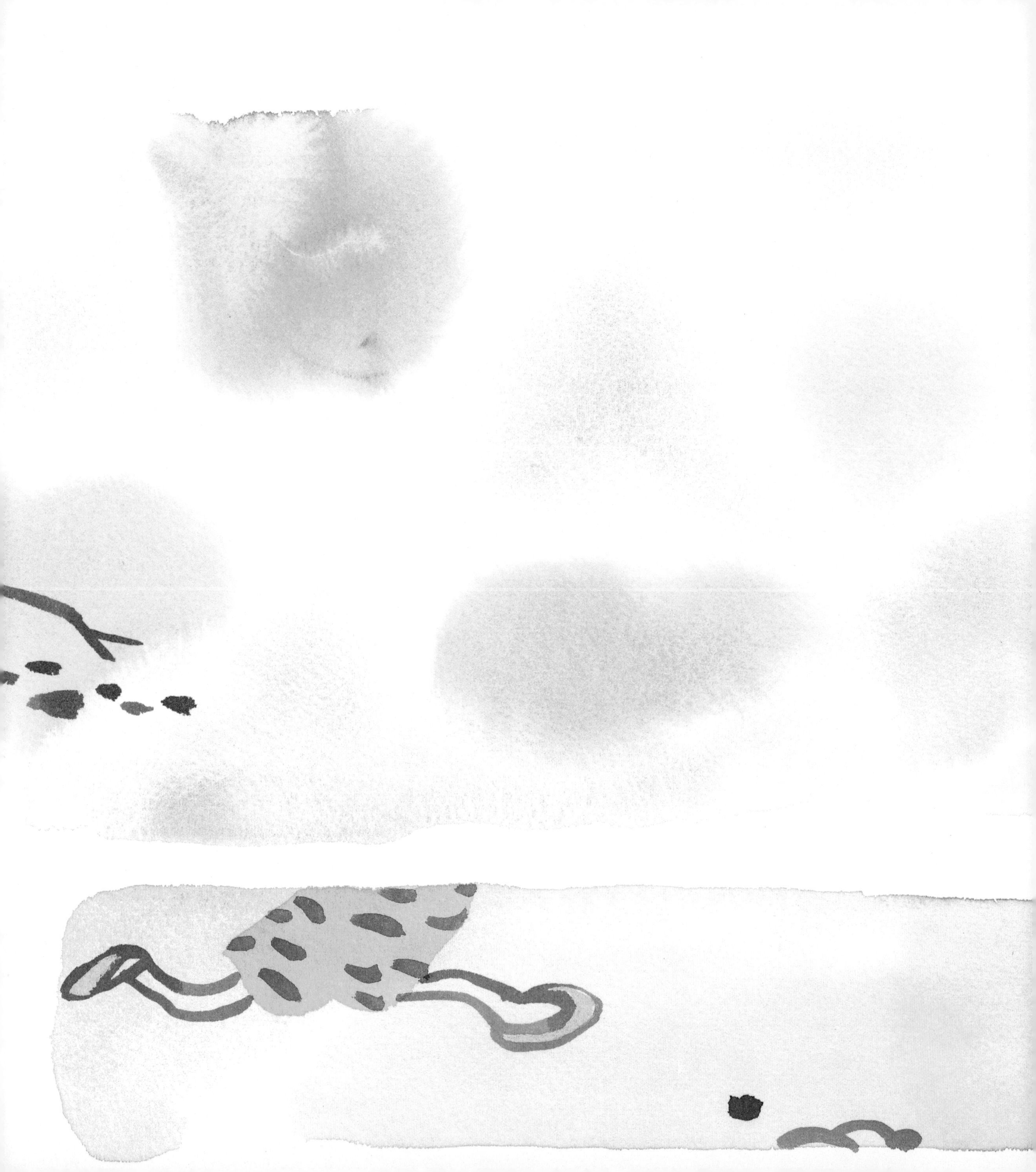

Central Islip Public Library
33 Hawthorne Avenue
Central Islip, NY 11722-2498

HM SEP 15 2011 ✓

CENTRAL ISLIP PUBLIC LIBRARY
3 1800 00280 3274

280 3274

JE Raschka, Christopher
RAS

A Ball for Daisy

$16.95

Central Islip Public Library
33 Hawthorne Avenue
Central Islip, NY 11722-2498

GAYLORD